Irving Browne, Jean Racine

The suitors

A comedy in three acts

Irving Browne, Jean Racine

The suitors
A comedy in three acts

ISBN/EAN: 9783337102098

Printed in Europe, USA, Canada, Australia, Japan

Cover: Foto ©Andreas Hilbeck / pixelio.de

More available books at **www.hansebooks.com**

THE

SUITORS:

A

COMEDY IN THREE ACTS.

TRANSLATED INTO ENGLISH VERSE FROM THE FRENCH OF

RACINE.

BY IRVING BROWNE,

OF THE TROY BAR.

NEW YORK:

G. P. PUTNAM & SONS.

1871.

THE NEW YORK PRINTING COMPANY,

81, 83, *and* 85 *Centre Street*,

NEW-YORK.

TO THOSE NOT OF MY PROFESSION, WHO LOVE A JEST AT OUR
EXPENSE, AND TO THOSE OF MY PROFESSION WHO CAN LAUGH AT
SUCH A JEST, I DEDICATE THIS TRANSLATION.

TRANSLATOR'S PREFACE.

SOME extracts from the following pages, including the Trial of the Dog, were originally published in a series of papers in the Albany Law Journal, on " Law and Lawyers in Literature." As I then wrote, I was not aware of any translation of this comedy into English. Shortly after, I received from LEVI BISHOP, Esq., of the Detroit Bar, a literal prose translation of the comedy, published by him in 1862. This suggested to me the idea of translating the entire play into English verse. I confess my obligations to Mr. BISHOP'S spirited rendering, and to some valuable hints derived from correspondence with him.

I have endeavored to make the translation as literal as possible; and have adopted verse, not on account of any poetical merit to be claimed for my verse, but because I thought it would enhance the absurdity and extravagance of the situations.

It is said that a troublesome and disastrous lawsuit, to which RACINE was a party, was the occasion of his writing this, his only comedy. As will be seen, by the Author's Preface, it is founded upon the " Wasps " of ARISTOPHANES.

It may be well to remind the reader of the significance of the names of some of the dramatist's characters. *Dandin* means simpleton; *Intimé*, appellee or respondent; *Chicaneau* is evidently from *chicaner*, to pettifog; *Pimbesche*, one of the Countess' titles, means impertinent minx.

TROY, *April,* 1870.

AUTHOR'S PREFACE.

WHEN I read the "Wasps" of ARISTOPHANES, I hardly imagined that I should construct from it "The Suitors." I confess that it amused me exceedingly, and that I found in it a great fund of humor, which tempted me to make it accessible to the public; but I had contemplated putting it into the Italian tongue, as a production which of clear right belonged to the genius of that people. The judge who leaped from his window, the criminal dog and the tears of his family, seemed to me incidents worthy of the gravity of SCARAMOUCH. The departure of that actor interrupted my design, and a desire arose among some of my friends to see on our theater a specimen of ARISTOPHANES. I did not yield to the first proposition which they made me; I told them that despite a certain humor which I had found in this author, my inclination would not lead me to take him for a model, if I were going to write a comedy; and that I should much prefer to imitate the regularity of MENANDER and of TERENCE, rather than the license of ARISTOPHANES and PLAUTUS. They replied that it was not a comedy that they required of me, and that they only wished to learn whether the wit of ARISTOPHANES would preserve its grace in our language. Therefore, partly by encouraging me, and partly by themselves putting my hand to the work, my friends compelled me to commence a piece which dragged but little in its completion.

Still, the greater part of the world have no heed for the design or the diligence of authors. At first they criticised that which was written for amusement, as if I had intended a tragedy. Even those who were the most diverted by it, were afraid lest they should laugh contrary to precedent, and found fault that I had not more seriously purposed to make them laugh. Some others imagined that it was decorous for them to be wearied by it, and that the affairs of the palace could not be a subject of diversion for courtiers. The piece was soon afterwards played at Versailles. They did not scruple to enjoy it there, and those who would have thought themselves disgraced by applauding it in Paris have perhaps been forced to laugh at Versailles, to keep themselves in countenance.

They are wrong who reproach me with fatiguing their ears with too much pettifoggery. It is a language more unfamiliar to me than to any one else; and I have used no barbarous words but such as I learned in court, in a suit which neither my judges nor myself have ever thoroughly understood.

If I have any thing to fear, it is that persons who are somewhat destitute of humor, will not tolerate the sportiveness of the trial of the dog, and the extravagancies of the judge. But after all, I translate Aristophanes; and they ought to remember that he was concerned with an audience rather exacting; the Athenians apparently knew what was true Attic salt, and they were well assured when they had laughed at any thing, that they had not applauded nonsense.

For my own part, I think Aristophanes was right in carrying his ideas beyond the bounds of probability. The judges of the Areopagus perhaps would not easily have discovered that he had satirized their natural avidity for gain, the clever tricks of their clerks, and the tediousness of their advocates. It was proper to exaggerate these personages a little, to enable them to recognize themselves; the public did not fail to discern the truth under the guise of ridicule; and I am sure it is better to have employed the irrelevant eloquence of two orators on the subject of an accused dog, than to have placed at the dock a veritable criminal, and to have interested the spectators in the life of a human being.

At all events, I can say that our age has not been less appreciative of humor than that of ARISTOPHANES, and that if the end of my comedy had been to excite laughter, comedy never more completely fulfilled its purpose. Not that I expect great honor for having so long amused the world, but I know that it was my wish to do it without using a single one of those indecent ambiguities or rude jocularities which are now so freely indulged in by the greater part of our authors, who have buried the theater in a degradation out of which chaster writers would lift it.

2

PERSONS REPRESENTED:

DANDIN, a judge whose wits are disordered.

LEANDRE, his son, a gay youth, in love with Isabelle.

CHICANEAU, a litigious burgess.

PETIT-JEAN, porter to Dandin, and illiterate.

L'INTIMÉ, secretary to Dandin.

A PROMPTER.

ISABELLE, Chicaneau's daughter, in love with Léandre.

COUNTESS, litigious.

SCENE — A city in Lower Normandy.

ACT FIRST.

SCENE I.

Petit-Jean, dragging a large bag of law papers:
He who in the future puts his trust is mad, I say;
Those who laugh on 'Friday will cry on Saturday.
Into his service a judge took me last year,—
To be his porter, from Amiens brought me here.
To raise a laugh at us these Normans always help,
But when with wolves, 'tis said, one quickly learns to
     yelp.
Although from Picardy, good sense I did not lack,
But with the best of them I made my whip to crack.
They spoke to me uncovered — the men of conse-
     quence —
'Twas " Mr. de Little-John " — how great their defer-
     ence !
But honor without money is a malady.
I was the model porter of a comedy.
No use for them to knock, and doff their hats to me,
No one gets in our house without the porter's fee.
No pay, no service — my door was shut the faster.
True, once in a while I accounted with my master,
And gave him something back. And I was always
     sent
To purchase hay and candles for the establishment,
But I lost naught by that. Indeed, for aught I saw,
I well might have afforded also to give the straw.
Twas pity that on business he'd so set his heart.

At court he was the first to come, last to depart,
And often all alone—such actions would you think ?—
He'd there lie down and sleep without his food or drink.
" Mr. Perrin-Dandin "—sometimes to him I've said,
" Truth is, you 're every day too early out of bed.
He who would travel far should ever spare his nag,
Eat, drink, and sleep—keep up spirits that never flag."
He took no heed.   He's so laborious, and in fact
So little sleep he takes, that many say he 's cracked.
First one and then another, to judge us all he 'd wish ;
He's always muttering over certain gibberish
That I don't understand.   And then, whate'er may hap,
He'll never sleep but in his gown and judicial cap.
Once he cut his rooster's head off, in a passion,
Because he waked him up later than his fashion ;
Saying that a suitor, whose action had not thriven,
Bribes in form of hush-money this poor creature'd
    given.
Poor man, he's done much better since that rare
    decision.
To all on business his son denies admission.
To watch him day and night and everywhere, 'tis
    needed,
For my good man is off to court unless he's heeded.
T' escape from us, at times he will be cheerful seen.
As for myself, I sleep no more.   I'm growing lean.
When I stretch myself, I can only yawn — heigho !
Let who will watch now, here is my pillow.
For one night, on my word, I'll sleep in self-defence.
To snooze here in the street there can be no offence.
Here goes.   (*Lies down on the ground.*)

SCENE II.

L'INTIMÉ, PETIT-JEAN.

L'Intimé :

Little-John, ho, Little-John!

Petit-Jean :

L'Intimé!

He is afraid that I have taken cold this way. (*Aside.*)

L'Intimé :

What the devil do you so early in the street?

Petit-Jean :

Is it necessary to stay there on one's feet,
Always to watch a man, and hear him yelling out?
What lungs he has! He is bewitched, beyond a doubt.

L'Intimé :

Good!

Petit-Jean :

Just now I said to him, rubbing up my hair,
That I would like to sleep. "Present thy formal prayer,
Whereas thou want'st to sleep," he said with gravity.
I fall asleep e'en now, only in telling thee.
Good-night.

L'Intimé :

But how good-night? What devil do I care,
If—but I hear a noise about the door up there.

SCENE III.

DANDIN, L'INTIMÉ, PETIT-JEAN.

Dandin, at the window :

Petit-Jean! L'Intimé!

L'Intimé to Petit-Jean:
Peace!
Dandin:
I am here alone.
My jailors then have made default, thank heaven, and
gone.
If I should give them time they would again appear,
So, to enlarge ourselves, we'll leap the window here.
Court is adjourned.
L'Intimé:
O, how he jumps!
Petit-Jean:
O, sir, you're caught.
Dandin:
Stop thief! Stop thief!
Petit-Jean:
O, we shall hold you as we ought.
L'Intimé:
No use of crying out, sir.
Dandin:
Help here, quick! I'm beat!

SCENE IV.

LEANDRE, DANDIN, L'INTIMÉ, PETIT-JEAN.
Léandre:
Quick, now, a light! I hear my father in the street.
My father, why go out at this untimely hour?
Where go you in the night?
Dandin:
I wish t'assert my power.

Léandre:

And over whom? All are asleep.

Petit-Jean:

In faith, I don't sleep much.

Léandre:

What bags of documents! His very knees they touch.

Dandin:

Within doors for three months I will not ask admission
Of actions and of bags I've made a great provision.

Léandre:

And who will feed you?

Dandin:

The inn-keeper, I suppose.

Léandre:

But father, where'll you sleep?

Dandin:

At court and in my clothes.

Léandre:

My father, it is better you shouldn't go out thus.
Sleep here, in your own house, and take your meals
    with us.
Suffer yourself to be by reason guided still,
And for your health —

Dandin:

Why, I prefer to be unwell.

Léandre:

You're that too much already. Take rest, for which
    you groan,
Or very soon you'll be reduced to skin and bone.

Dandin:

Rest! Ah, your father by yourself you'd regulate;

3

Do you suppose a judge does naught but hold high
    state?
To scour the streets like gay young men in their
    carouses?
To run to balls by day, by night to gaming-houses?
Money is not earned so fast in my dominion.
Each one of thy fine ribbons costs me 'n opinion.
My gown makes you ashamed! And you a judge's
    son!
Would'st act the gentleman? Oh, fie, Dandin, have
    done!
Consider in my wardrobe and in my sleeping room
The portraits of the Dandins; all these have worn the
    gown.
It is a good profession. Compare, too, price for price,
The New Year gifts of a good judge, and those of a
    marquis.
Remark what we shall be at the end of next Decem-
    ber:—
What's then your gentleman? A post in the ante-
    chamber.
How many a one of these, the proudest, you've seen
    linger
About my audience, and there to blow his finger,
Or hand in pocket, cloak on nose; finally to sit
And warm himself a while by turning at my spit.
This is the way one treats such folks. Ah, my poor
    lad,
Have you such inculcations from your dead mother
    had?
Poor Babonette! As I recall to memory,

She never failed at every term of court to be.
Never, no, never, would she leave me for a day,
And heaven only knows what oft she brought away.
Rather than empty-handed to our house return,
The very napkins at the inn she would not spurn.
This is the way fine houses are fixed up.   Oh, you
Will always be a fool.

Léandre :

Come, you'll be frozen through,
My father.   Little John, conduct your master back,
Put him to bed ; in door and window leave no crack;
Let all be fastened, so he be from cold protected.

Petit-Jean :

Cause then at least a railing there to be erected.

Dandin :

What ! shall I be sent to bed in fashion thus abnormal ?
Obtain an order that I sleep, in manner formal.

Léandre :

For once, my father, lie down in any fashion.

Dandin :

I'll go, but I intend to put you in a passion.
I will not go to sleep.

Léandre :

Oh, well, that's all in vain.
Don't leave him here alone.   You, L'Intimé, remain.

SCENE V.

LÉANDRE, L'INTIMÉ.

Léandre :

I wish to speak with you a moment here alone.

L'Intimé :

What! must you needs be guarded?

Léandre :

   That I well may own.
Alas! I have my weakness well as my father.

L'Intimé :

Oh, you would judge, then?

Léandre, pointing to the house of Isabelle :

   Seek there the mystery rather.
You know that house?

L'Intimé :

   I understand you now at last.
The dickens! Cupid has untimely got you fast.
Undoubtedly you'd speak to me of Isabelle.
A hundred times I've said, she's wise, she looks quite
  well;
But Mr. Chicaneau, you surely ought t' have pondered,
The greater part of his estate in law has squandered;
Whom does he not prosecute? I believe all France,
Unless he dies, in court will be compelled to dance.
Hard by the judge he's taken up his residence;
One forever sues, the other passes sentence.
Before your affair is done, the chances are that he
Will sue the parson, son-in-law, and notary.

Léandre :

I know it well as you, but spite of all, oh, how, sir,
I pine for Isabelle.

L'Intimé :

   Well, then, why not espouse her?
Nothing to do but speak—no need of preparation.

Léandre:

But things move not so fast as your imagination.
Her father is a savage whom I greatly fear.
None but a bailiff, sergeant, or solicitor
Can ever see his daughter; the poor Isabelle,
Imprisoned in her house, laments invisible;
In grief she sees her youthful freshness dissipate,
In smoke my passion, and in lawsuits his estate.
She'll utterly be ruined unless he is restrained.
Do you not know some honest forger, to be gained
To serve his friends—for compensation, understand—
Some zealous sergeant?

L'Intimé:

Many such at your command.

Léandre:

But still?

L'Intimé:

Oh, sir, if my deceased, lamented sire
Were still alive, he would accomplish your desire.
He'd do more in a day than some in half a year.
Graven in wrinkles on his face did writs appear.
He would arrest for you the carriage of a prince,
And nab the prince himself; and if in any province,
One of his bailiffs caught twenty castigations,
Father took nineteen-twentieths of the compensations.
But what do you require? Am I not the master's son?
I'll serve you.

Léandre:

You?

L'Intimé:

Better than a sergeant would have done.

Léandre:

You'd carry to the father a forged writ?

L'Intimé:

No doubt.

Léandre:

And give this billet to the daughter?

L'Intimé:

Yes, why not?

I'm up to both.

Léandre:

I hear a noise; come now, — I see;
We'll elsewhere go and regulate our scheme.

SCENE VI.

CHICANEAU, PETIT-JEAN.

Chicaneau, going and returning:

La Brie,
Let the house be guarded, I soon will home repair.
Don't permit a person to go above the stair.
Convey this letter bound to Maine unto the post,
And from my warren take three rabbits fit to roast,
And carry them to my solicitor to-day.
Make his clerk taste my wine if he should come this
      way.
Deliver him the bag that's in my room suspended.
Is that all?   To visit me there perhaps intended
A certain tall, gaunt man who gets me evidence,
And swears himself whenever I am at a pinch;
Let him await.   I fear my judge is out.   The clock
Has sounded four.   We'll go and at his entrance knock

Petit-Jean, opening the door :

Who's there?

Chicaneau :

Can I his honor see?

Petit-Jean, shutting the door :

No.

Chicaneau, knocking :

Well, can't I then

Say a word to Mr. Secretary?

Petit-Jean, shutting the door :

No, again.

Chicaneau, knocking :

And Mr. Porter?

Petit-Jean :

That's myself.

Chicaneau, giving him money :

Ah, drink my health,

I pray you, sir.

Petit-Jean, taking the money :

Thanks, sir, and may you long have wealth,
(*Shutting the door*) But come again to-morrow.

Chicaneau :

My money then restore.

Truly, this world is growing wicked more and more.
I 've seen the time when suits did not disturb one's ease;
You'd buy a half a dozen for a crown apiece.
But now-a-days my whole estate is hardly more
Than would suffice to buy the porter at the door.
But madam the countess of Pimbesche approaches—
Affairs of haste, I think, from the way she rushes.

SCENE VII.

COUNTESS, CHICANEAU.

Chicaneau :

Madam, there's no admittance.

Countess :

　　　　　　　　Just as I prophesied.

To speak the truth, my servants will drive me soon
　beside

Myself; to get them out of bed, in vain I scold;

And every day I have to wake them, young and old.

Chicaneau :

T' conceal himself he finds it indispensable.

Countess :

To speak to him these two days I've not been able.

Chicaneau :

My adversary 's strong; I 've every thing to dread.

Countess :

After what 's done to me, no use to ope my head.

Chicaneau :

If, however, I am right—

Countess :

　　　　　　　　O sir, such decrees !

Chicaneau :

I 'll submit my case to you.   Listen, if you please.

Countess :

That you may see their baseness, sir, let me relate—

Chicaneau :

At bottom there is really nothing—

Countess :

　　　　　　　　Let me state—

Chicaneau :

Here are the facts : Fifteen or twenty years an ass
Over my meadow had accustomed been to pass
And there disport himself, by which much waste he
    made,
For which before the village judge my plaint I laid.
The ass I attach.   The appraiser's nominated,
At trusses two of hay the waste is estimated.
In short, with this award, after a year, they fling
Me empty out of court.   And then an appeal I bring.
Now while th' appeal in court was sleeping at its ease, —
Remark particularly, madame, if you please,—
My lawyer, Drolichon—no fool—on my petition,
Obtained by bribery a premature decision,
And thus I gain my cause.   On that, what next is
    done ?
My adversary stays the execution.
But while procedure on procedure thickens,
My adversary lets in my field his chickens.
To ascertain, unto the court it then seemed meet,
How much of grass one chicken in one day can eat.
Issue at last is joined.   In fine, when every thing
In that condition stands, the cause they say they 'll
    bring
To 'n end, April fifteenth or sixteenth, 'fifty-six.
I write fresh score.   I furnish evidence, and mix
Plaints, pleas and inquests, inspections compulsory,
Appraisals, transfers, three interlocutory
Orders, and grievances, fresh acts, reports, *res gestæ ;*
I forge my name in letters issued by Majesty ;
Fourteen appointments, twenty writs, six allegations,

4

Productions six and twenty, twenty just'fications,
Judgment in short.   My cause is swallowed in expense
Amounting to about five or six thousand francs.
Call you this doing right?   Is this the way they
    adjudge?
After fifteen or twenty years!   There's one refuge,—
The petition civil,—that still remains to me.
I am not quite defeated.   But you, too, I see,
Are litigating?

Countess:

Would to heaven!

Chicaneau:

My books I'll burn.

Countess:

I—

Chicaneau:

Six thousand francs!   Of hay, two trusses in return!

Countess:

Sir, all my litigations they're seeking to restrain;
Four or five small issues are all that now remain;
One suit against my husband, and another suit
Against my father and my children; why they do't
I know not, nor can tell what woes they have de-
    nounced
Against me, miserable; but they have pronounced
This judgment: that, supplied with food and clothing
    due,
For th' balance of my life I am forbid to sue.

Chicaneau:

To sue?

Countess:

To sue.

Chicaneau.:
Truly, this is a dark affair.
I'm much surprised at it.
Countess:
I'm driven to despair.
Chicaneau:
To treat nobility as if of no account.
But your allowance, madam, is of some amount?
Countess:
To manage to exist on it, no doubt I can sir,
But living without law, for me will never answer.
Chicaneau:
With our life-blood these folks will pamper their
digestion,
And we can't say a word! But, if it's a fair question,
How long have you been lawing?
Countess:
My memory is not clear.
Some thirty years or more.
Chicaneau:
Why, that's not long.
Countess:
Oh, dear!
Chicaneau:
And how old may you be? You have a healthful
visage.
Countess:
Oh, some sixty years.
Chicaneau:
Indeed! why, for lawsuits, this age
Is best of all.

Countess:

Well, let them work, they've not yet done.
I'll sell my last chemise.   I will have all or none.

Chicaneau:

Now, madam, listen to me.   This is what you must do.

Countess:

Yes, sir, as if my father, I will believe in you.

Chicaneau:

I would go unto my judge.

Countess:

Oh, yes, sir, I will go.

Chicaneau:

And throw myself before him.

Countess:

Myself I there will throw;
I'm quite resolved on that.

Chicaneau:

But now attend to me.

Countess:

Oh, yes, you take the thing just as it ought to be.

Chicaneau:

Have you got through now ?

Countess:

Yes.

Chicaneau:

Then, to my judge I would
Proceed informally.

Countess:

This gentleman 's so good !

Chicaneau:

If *you* talk all the time, I must preserve my peace.

Countess :

I'm very much obliged.   I feel quite at my ease.

Chicancau :

I'd go and find my judge, and say to him—

Countess :

Yes—

Chicaneau :

Mind me—

And I would say to him, My Lord—

Countess :

Yes, sir—

Chicaneau :

Bind me—

Countess :

I don't wish to be bound, sir.

Chicaneau :

Nothing of the sort.

Countess :

And I will not be bound.

Chicaneau :

Why, now, you're full of sport.

Countess :

No.

Chicaneau :

But, madam, you can't see what I'm driving at.

Countess :

I must litigate, sir, or never can do that.

Chicaneau :

But—

Countess :

Again I tell you, sir, I will not be bound.

Chicaneau :

Now truly, when a woman's intellect's unsound —

Countess :

You're mad yourself.

Chicaneau :

Madam !

Countess :

For what should they bind me ?

Chicaneau :

But, madam —

Countess :

See the man's familiarity !

Chicaneau :

But, madam —

Countess :

Full of his tricks, this dirty fellow'd pass
For a wise counselor !

Chicaneau :

Madam !

Countess :

With his young ass !

Chicaneau :

You drive me mad !

Countess :

Good man, go home and watch your grass.

Chicaneau :

You weary me.

Countess :

The fool !

Chicaneau :

No witness near, alas !

SCENE VIII.

PETIT-JEAN, COUNTESS, CHICANEAU.

Petit-Jean :

What a disturbance they are making at our gate.
Move on, sirs, if you wish to clamor at this rate.

Chicaneau :

Sir, I call you to witness —

Countess :

This fellow is a fool.

Chicaneau :

You hear her, sir; remember this word against all rule.

Petit-Jean, to Countess :

T' escape you such expressions you ought not to allow.

Countess :

Indeed! it's right for him to call me mad just now.

Petit-Jean, to Chicaneau :

Mad! you say wrong, sir. Why thus her feelings
wound ?

Chicaneau :

I only counseled her.

Petit-Jean :

Oh !

Countess :

Yes, to have me bound !

Petit-Jean :

Oh, sir !

Chicanean :

Why won't the woman hear me to the end ?

Petit-Jean :

Oh, madam !

Countess :

Who ? am I to help this man contend ?

Chicaneau :

A prying woman !

Petit- Jean :

Oh, be still !

Countess :

Trickster !

Petit- Jean :

Stop, do !

Chicaneau :

Who dares no more to litigate ?

Countess :

What 's that to you ?
Make what you can of it, forger abominable,
You thief, you mischief-maker !

Chicaneau :

Good, good ! oh, the devil !
Sergeant, ho ! a sergeant !

Countess :

Bailiff ! a bailiff here !

Petit- Jean :

In faith, they all need binding—suitors and judge—I
fear.

ACT SECOND.

SCENE I.

LÉANDRE, L'INTIMÉ.

L'Intimé :

Once more—that I should do the whole, it is not fair ;
While I act bailiff, do you play commissioner.
You 've but to follow me, in robe redundant ;
You 'll find the means to talk with her abundant.
Exchange for darker locks your wig of flaxen hair.
These suitors—will they dream who in the world you
    are ?
Ah, when unto your father they go their court to pay,
You hardly even know whether it yet is day.
But this litigious countess do you not admire ?—
To throw whom in my way good fortune did conspire ?
Who, when she thought she saw me taken in the snare,
To Chicaneau has bid me with this writ repair,
Assigning certain words as grounds of her attack,
By which he sought to make her out a maniac ;
Mad, I say,—to be bound, and for other violence
And blasphemies, always of suits the ornaments.
But you have nought remarked of all my equipage.
Of a sergeant havn't I the face and carriage ?

Léandre :

Ah, very well !

L'Intimé :

    Since morning, violence to suffer,
I feel in soul and body six times tougher.

5

Let come what will, the writ is here, your letter there;
That Isabelle shall have the latter, I will swear.
But to get executed this contract which you see,
It's needful, close upon my heels you should follow me ;
Pretending to inquire into all the matter,
Under her father's nose make love directly at her.

Léandre :

But don't make love to father, and the daughter sue.

L'Intimé :

Father shall have the writ, daughter the billet-doux.
Let's enter.

(Knocks at Isabelle's door.)

SCENE II.

ISABELLE, L'INTIMÉ.

Isabelle :

Who knocks ?

L'Intimé :

A friend. (Aside.) The voice of Isabelle.

Isabelle :

Do you require to see some one, sir ?

L'Intimé :

Mad'moiselle,

I have for you a trifling process, and I pray,
Honor me by taking it in the legal way.

Isabelle :

Excuse me, sir, these matters I don't understand ;
Father will soon be here, whom you can then command,

L'Intimé :

He's not within then, now, Miss ?

Isabelle :
No ; he's not arrived.

L'Intimé :
The summons, Miss, it seems, with your own name's
inscribed.

Isabelle :
I have no doubt, sir, you mistake me for another.
Without having lawsuits, their cost I can discover ;
If every one like me detested litigation,
The like of you would seek some other occupation.
Good-bye.

L'Intimé :
Permit me —

Isabelle :
There's nothing I'll permit you.

L'Intimé :
It's not a summons.

Isabelle :
Nonsense !

L'Intimé :
It's a billet-doux.

Isabelle :
Still less then.

L'Intimé :
But peruse it.

Isabelle :
You cannot thus cheat me.

L'Intimé :
From Mr. ——

Isabelle :
Good-bye.

L'Intimé :
Léander.
Isabelle :
Speak in a lower key.
This is from Mr. —?
L'Intimé :
Deuce take it ! I'm quite out of breath.
To be heard, one's got to talk himself almost to death !
Isabelle :
Ah ! L'Intime ! but please, my 'stonished senses
pardon.
Give 't here.
L'Intimé :
But then my nose you'd shut the door quite
hard on ?
Isabelle :
Who would have known you, now, disguised in that
condition ?
Give 't me.
L'Intimé :
Then does your door give honest folks
admission ?
Isabelle :
Oh, give it up !
L'Intimé :
The pest !
Isabelle :
Well, then, if you think better,
You may retrace your footsteps, and retain your letter.
L'Intimé :
Here 'tis. Another time use more consideration.

SCENE III.

CHICANEAU, ISABELLE, L'INTIMÉ.

Chicaneau :

I'm a fool and thief then, in her estimation!
A sergeant's charged to thank her for the compliment;
And a dish of my own cooking has to her been sent.
I should be very sorry had this been otherwise,
And if with prior summons she should me surprise.
How now? Does any man about my daughter hover?
See, now, she reads a letter! Ah! 'tis from some
    lover.
Let us approach.

                Isabelle :

          Shall I believe?   Can I suppose
Your master is sincere?

             L'Intimé :

           He takes no more repose
Than your father; frets himself; he'll — (*perceiving
    Chicaneau*) this day make it plain,
That even if you sue him, you nothing have to gain.

       Isabelle, seeing Chicaneau :

It is my father! (*To L'Intimé.*) Well, sir, you may
    tell your client,
That if he perseveres, he'll find us still defiant.
Here now, you may behold, sir, how your writ is used.
    (*Tears the letter.*)

           Chicaneau :

What, then! it was a summons that my girl perused!
Some day you'll be the honor of your family,

My life, my daughter, you'll defend your property.
Come, I will buy for you the code of practice civil.
But tearing up law-writs will never do — the devil !

Isabelle, to L'Intimé:

Assure them, I have little fear of them, in short;
And let them do their worst, they only make me sport.

Chicaneau:

Ah ! don't get angry.

Isabelle, to L'Intimé:

Good bye, sir, to you.

SCENE IV.

CHICANEAU, L'INTIMÉ.

L'Intimé, taking a position to write:

Now come,

Let's have the facts.

Chicaneau:

Pray, pardon her.   How business's done,
She has not been instructed.   Besides, sir, if you please,
Behold ! I can the pieces together put with ease.

L'Intimé:

No.

Chicaneau:

I can read it well.

L'Intimé:

It's of no consequence,
I have a copy with me.

Chicaneau:

Ah ! that countenance
Impresses me — but strangely, the longer I reflect

Upon your face, it seems to me the less I recollect.
I know so many bailiffs.

L'Intimé :

About me, sir, inquire.
In my small way I well discharge what you require.

Chicaneau :

May be. Whom do you represent ?

L'Intimé :

A lady, sir, of rank,
Who greatly reverences you, and from her soul would
thank
You, if you'd condescend to answer my citation,
And give her but a single word of reparation.

Chicaneau :

Of reparation ? Surely, I've done no one harm.

L'Intimé :

I can believe you, sir. You have a heart too warm.

Chicaneau :

What then do you require ?

L'Intimé :

She wishes, sir, that you,
Before some witnesses, would her the honor do
T' avow that she's quite sane, and not demented.

Chicaneau :

My countess !

L'Intimé :

To remain your servant she's contented.

Chicaneau :

I'm hers, to be commanded.

L'Intimé :

The proffer, sir,
Is kind.

Chicaneau :

Yes, please assure her that an officer
From me shall bear to her all for which she contends.
What now! The beaten, on my faith, must make
   amends!
Let's see what she says here: "Sixth of January,
For having falsely said it was necessary,—
Being thereto induced by the spirit of chicane—
To bind that high and mighty dame, Yolande Cudasne,
Countess of Pimbesche and Orbesche, and so forth,
It's ordered that immediately he go forth,
Unto the lady's lodgings, and there in clear voice, he—
In presence of four witnesses and a notary—"
Oh pshaw !—"said Hierome shall openly admit
That he esteems her sound in mind, and of good wit.
LE BON." This of your seigniory is then the title ?

L'Intimé :

The same, to serve you, sir. (*Aside.*) To brass it out
   is vital.

Chicaneau :

LE BON ! Writs signed that way have never been in
   vogue.
Mr. Le Bon—

L'Intimé :

Well, sir.

Chicaneau :

I think you are a rogue.

L'Intimé :

I beg your pardon, sir, I am an honest man.

Chicaneau :

But the most arrant knave from Rome to Caen.

L'Intimé :

Well, sir, 'tis not for me your notion to gainsay,
But you 'll have the pleasure roundly for this to pay.

Chicaneau :

I pay? In blows.

L'Intimé :

You 're too polite, such pains to take.
But you shall pay me well.

Chicaneau :

You cause my head to ache.
Take that—that is your pay. (*Striking him.*)

L'Intimé :

A blow! Let's write it down:
" After a great resistance, aforesaid Hierome.
Did strike, to wit, did hit, my sergeant on the chop,
With the said blow causing his hat in the mud to
    drop."

Chicaneau :

Add that. (*Kicking him.*)

L'Intimé :

Good! The damages seem to accumulate.
I need this very much. " With this not satiate,
Aforesaid blows reiterated with a kick."
Courage! " More beside: aforesaid, in passion quick,
The present written statement tried to lacerate."
Come, that's not bad, dear sir. Why do you hesitate?
Don't give it up so soon.

Chicaneau :

You rogue!

L'Intimé :

And, if it please ye,

A few blows with a stick will make my income easy.

      Chicaneau, threatening him with a stick:

Indeed! I'll see if he's a sergeant true.

      L'Intimé, in position to write:

                So, sir,

Strike on.   I have four children to support.

      Chicaneau:

                Oh, sir,

Your pardon; for a sergeant you I'd never take;
But his wit sometimes the cleverest will forsake.
I'll make apology for this surmise outrageous.
Yes, you are sergeant, sir, and sergeant most coura
    geous.
Your hand; the like of you are such as I revere;
And I was educated always in the fear
Of God and of the sergeants, by my father late.

      L'Intimé:

No, one can't flog people at such a trifling rate.

      Chicaneau:

Oh, sir, spare me the law.

      L'Intimé:

           Your servant.   Contumacious,

A cudgel raised, a cuff, a kick, ah ha!

      Chicaneau:

              Oh, gracious!

Pray pay me off in kind.

      L'Intimé:

      That they were dealt suffices.

They're worth to me a thousand crowns, by last
    advices.

SCENE V.

LÉANDRE, IN A COMMISSIONER'S GOWN; CHICA-
NEAU, L'INTIMÉ.

L'Intimé :

Here in the nick of time comes the commissionary.
Oh, sir, your presence here is very necessary.
This man, as you may see, of a most violent
Buffet in the face made me a little present.

Léandre :

To you, sir ?

L'Intimé :

Yes, to me, speaking in proper person.
Item, a kick. Likewise, some names, to my aversion.

Léandre :

Have you some evidence of this ?

L'Intimé :

Why, sir, just feel it;
My cheek, still burning with the blow, will sure re-
veal it.

Léandre :

A criminal affair; and in the act detected.

Chicaneau :

Woe 's me !

L'Intimé :

His daughter, too — at least, one so suspected —
Has torn one of my papers all to bits, declaring
I gave her satisfaction, and with scornful bearing
She offers us defiance.

Léandre to L'Intimé :

Cause her to come to me.
A contumacious spirit reigns in this family.

Chicaneau, aside:

It's absolutely certain that I am bewitched.
If I know any of them, let my neck be stretched.

Léandre:

What! strike an officer!   But here's the rogue
inhuman.

SCENE VI.

ISABELLE, LÉANDRE, CHICANEAU, L'INTIMÉ.

L'Intimé to Isabelle:

Do you not recognize him?

Léandre:

Very well, young woman.
It's you then who have braved our man so naughtily,
And who have dared defy our power so haughtily?
Your name, now?

Isabelle:

Isabelle.

Léandre:

Your age, young lady?

Isabelle:

Eighteen.

Chicaneau:

I think she is a little on the shady
Side—no matter.

Léandre:

And are you with a mate provided?

Isabelle:

No, sir.

Léandre :

You seem to smile.   Set down that she derided.

(*To L'Intimé.*)

Chicaneau :

Of husbands, sir, to daughters, don't you chatter,
You see, such secrets are a family matter.

Léandre :

Put down, he interrupts.

Chicaneau :

Of that I never thought.

My daughter, take good care to answer as you ought.

Léandre :

Oh, don't be discomposed, but answer at your leisure,
There's nought we wish to do that can give you dis
pleasure.

Have you not just received from this officer in sight,
A certain paper writing ?

Isabelle :

Certainly sir.

Chicaneau :

That's right.

Léandre :

Well, did you tear this paper without perusal ?

Isabelle :

I did peruse it, please you.

Chicaneau :

Good !

Léandre to L'Intimé :

Write as usual.

Why then did you destroy it ?   (*To Isabelle.*)

Isabelle :
Because I was afraid,
To lay th' affair to heart my father would be made.
And that by reading it he'd greatly be annoyed.

Chicaneau :
Thus is pure naughtiness.   Thus process you'd avoid ?

Léandre :
You did not then destroy it out of willfulness ?
Or in contempt of those who in it you address ?

Isabelle :
For them I neither scorn nor anger entertain.

Léandre to L'Intimé :
Write that.

Chicaneau :
That she is like her father, sir, is plain.
She answers very well, sir.

Léandre :
Yet, you still exhibit
'Gainst those who wear the gown an evident bad
spirit.

Isabelle :
To me the robe has hitherto been an aversion,
But now I rapidly experience a conversion.

Chicaneau :
Poor child !   Come, come, as soon as it is in my power,
I'll mate you well, provided I escape the dower.

Léandre :
You anxiously desire that justice be appeased ?

Isabelle :
I'd rather anything than to have you displeased.

L'Intimé :

Sign, sir.

Léandre :

I trust, at least, where'er we have it,
You will corroborate your affidavit ?

Isabelle :

Rest assured, sir, Isabelle by her word will stand.

Léandre :

Sign, then. That's well. Justice can nothing more
    demand.
Come, don't you also sign, sir ? (*To Chicaneau.*)

Chicaneau :

Oh yes, most willingly.
I subscribe what she has said, unhesitatingly.

Léandre, in a low tone to Isabelle :

Every thing goes bravely on, and as I designed,
A legal contract, written in due form, he's signed,
And he will be condemned by his own signature.

Chicaneau :

He's taken with her wit. What's he saying to her ?

Léandre :

Discreet as you are beautiful remain, and you
Will find all well. Bailiff, conduct her home. Adieu !
And you, sir, march yourself. (*To Chicaneau.*)

Chicaneau :

Where, sir ?

Léandre :

Just follow me.

Chicaneau :

Whither ?

Léandre:

You'll find.   Come, in the name of majesty.

Chicaneau:

How now!

SCENE VII.

LÉANDRE, CHICANEAU, PETIT-JEAN.

Petit-Jean:

Has no one seen my master there? — hallo!
Which way did he go out?   By the door or window?

Léandre:

What next?

Petit-Jean:

I cannot tell what's happened to his son;
The father's gone where destined by the evil one.
For spices — perquisites — incessantly he howled,
And, unsuspecting, I about the kitchen prowled
To find the pepper-bottle, and behind my back
He's disappeared.

SCENE VIII.

DANDIN, at a dormer window; LÉANDRE, CHICAN-
EAU, L'INTIMÉ, PETIT-JEAN.

Dandin:

Peace, peace!   Why don't they stop that clack?

Léandre:

Oh, gracious heav'n!

Petit-Jean:
Look there! my faith! he's on the roof.

Dandin:
What folks are you down there? And what is your
behoof?
And who are you in gowns? — lawyers, or I'm in error.
Come, speak.

Petit-Jean :
You'll find that to the cats he'll carry terror.

Dandin :
To see my secretary did you take precaution?
Go first and ask him if I understand your motion.

Léandre :
That I should force him from that place is urgent.
Keep a sharp look-out on your prisoner, sergeant.

Petit-Jean :
Oh! ho!

Léandre :
If you'd preserve your physical condition,
Keep still and follow me.

SCENE IX.

Countess, Dandin, Chicaneau, L'Intimé.

Dandin:
Now quick, state your petition.

Chicaneau:
Sir, without your warrant they took me prisoner.
7

Countess:

Good heav'n! In the cock-loft I perceive his honor!
What is he doing there?

L'Intimé:

He's holding audience.
The field is clear for you.

Chicaneau:

They do me violence,
Your honor,—injure me, and therefore I come here
To enter my complaint.

Countess:

To make complaint I appear.

Chicaneau and Countess:

My adversary, sir, you see before you placed.

L'Intimé:

Zounds! In this inquiry I wish to be embraced.

Chicaneau, Countess, L'Intimé:

My lord, I come before you on a trifling matter.

Chicaneau:

Now, sirs, to state our rights one at a time is better.

Countess:

His rights! All that he states is nothing but deception.

Dandin:

What have they done?

Chicaneau, Countess, L'Intimé:

He's slandered me beyond conception.

L'Intimé:

Besides a blow, your honor, which makes me most
abused.

Chicaneau:

Your honor, I am cousin to one of your nephews.

Countess :

By Father Cordon, sir, my action will be stated.

L'Intimé :

To your apothecary, sir, I am related.

Dandin :

Your titles?

Countess :

I am countess.

L'Intimé :

Bailiff.

Chicaneau :

I'm citizen.

Gentlemen—

Dandin, retiring from the window :

Proceed; I'll hear all three together then.

Chicaneau :

Gentlemen—

L'Intimé :

See there, he's off! Our chance diminishes.

Countess :

Alas!

Chicaneau :

Ah, what! Is it thus the session finishes?
I haven't had a chance two words yet to disclose.

SCENE X.

LÉANDRE without his gown; CHICANEAU, COUNTESS, L'INTIMÉ.

Léandre :

Gentlemen, be good enough to leave us in repose.

Chicaneau :

Can any one come in, sir ?

Léandre :

Not till I die first.

Chicaneau :

Alas ! But why ? In one small hour, or two at worst,
I'd finish.

Léandre :

But I say, we can't receive a caller.

Countess :

It's well to shut the door against that brawler.
But I —

Léandre :

No one can enter, I assure you still.

Countess :

Oh, sir, but I will enter.

Léandre :

Perhaps.

Countess :

I'm sure I will.

Léandre :

How ? through the window ?

Countess :

The door.

Léandre :

That 's to be tried.

Chicaneau :

Although until this evening I remain outside —

SCENE XI.

LÉANDRE, CHICANEAU, COUNTESS, L'INTIMÉ,
PETIT-JEAN.

Petit-Jean to Léandre:
No matter what we do, they do not seem to mind.
Zounds! in our lower room I have the judge confined,
Quite near the cellar.
                    Léandre:
                            Now then, once and forever,
Father shall not be seen.
                    Chicaneau:
                            Ah, well! If, however,
It is necessary that I should see him more—
        (*Dandin appears at an air-hole.*)
What do I see?   'Tis he whom heaven doth restore!
                    Léandre:
What! At the air-hole?
                    Petit-Jean:
                            He 's possessed, beyond a doubt.
                    Chicaneau:
Sir—
                    Dandin:
        Impertinent! But for you I should be out.
                    Chicaneau:
Your honor—
                    Dandin:
                            You 're a fool. Go, get you back.
                    Chicaneau:
My lord, will you not be so good —

Dandin :

> My head you 'll crack.

Chicaneau :

Sir, I have directed —

Dandin :

> Keep still, you are commanded.

Chicaneau :

There should be sent to you —

Dandin :

> To jail he is remanded.

Chicaneau :

Some quarter casks of wine.

Dandin :

> But I'll never listen to 't.

Chicaneau :

It is the best of muscat.

Dandin :

> Explain again your suit.

Léandre to L'Intimé :

We must surround them on all sides, with celerity.

Countess :

That which he speaks is full, sir, of insincerity.

Chicaneau :

Oh, sir, I speak the truth.

Dandin :

> Now let her tell her tale.

Countess :

Hear me, your honor.

Dandin :

> Oh, my breath begins to fail.

Chicaneau:

My lord—

Dandin:

You stifle me.

Countess:

Then hither turn your eye.

Dandin:

She stifles me. Oh, oh!

Chicaneau:

You're dragging me; oh, my!

Take care, I'm falling!

Petit-Jean:

There they go, upon my word,

Down in the cellar, all!

Léandre:

Fly! quick as any bird;

Hasten to their relief. But I at least suggest,

That Mr. Chicaneau, since he's down there, would best

Remain there all the day. See to it, L'Intimé.

L'Intimé:

You watch the air-hole, then.

L'andre:

I will. Quick now! I say.

SCENE XII.

COUNTESS, LÉANDRE.

Countess:

The wretch! He would his honor's judgment preju-
dice.

(*Through the air-hole.*) Don't you believe him, sir,
when he alleges this.
He's not a single witness. He's only lying.

Léandre :

What are you telling them ? Perhaps they're dying.

Countess:

Oh, sir, he'll make him credit any thing he'll choose.
Oh, let me enter.

Léandre :

No, ma'am, that I must refuse.

Countess:

The present of that wine, 'tis easily detected,
The judgment of the son and father has infected.
Patience ! As may be needful I'll protest, and ask
Relief against his lordship and the quarter-cask.

Léandre :

Go then, and cease to give us so much worriment.
What maniacs ! I've never seen such merriment.

SCENE XIII.

DANDIN, LÉANDRE, L'INTIMÉ.

L'Intimé :

My lord, where are you going ? Of danger you make
sport,
And yet you're limping badly.

Dandin :

I'm going to hold court.

Father, how now ? To dress your wounds give us
    permission.
A surgeon call.

Dandin :

He may attend me at the session.

Léandre :

But oh ! my father, stay —

Dandin :

Oh, I can see through you ;
That which suits your purpose you think to make me
    do.
You seem to have neither love nor reverence for me.
I'm not permitted now to render a decree.
Complete your work, then. Quickly take this bag.

Léandre :

Go easy,
My father. Here's a chance to compromise, an 't
    please ye.
If without holding court existence is but anguish,
If to render justice, continually you languish,
Still, 'tis unnecessary far abroad to roam,
But exercise your talents in a court at home.

Dandin :

You should not satirize the magistrates severely.
I wish to be a judge not in appearance merely.

Léandre :

On the other hand, you shall be judge without appeal,
With jurisdiction civil and criminal as well.
And every day two sessions you can hold with ease ;

At home do nothing else but render your decrees.
A servant fails to give a tumbler a good washing—
Condemn him to a fine; if broken, to a thrashing.

Dandin :

In this there's something, surely. Your reasoning's
    exquisite.
But then, again—will any pay me my perquisite?

Léandre :

You can detain their wages as security.

ʃ Dandin :

It seems to me he's talking very sensibly.

Léandre :

Against one of your neighbors—

SCENE XIV

DANDIN, LÉANDRE, L'INTIMÉ, PETIT-JEAN.

Petit-Jean :

Stop! Stop him! Catch him, do!

Léandre to L'Intimé :

Ah, 'tis my prisoner, without doubt, who's escaped
    from you.

L'Intimé :

No, no, fear nothing.

Petit-Jean :

All is lost. Your dog, Citron,
Has been and of our capon left nothing but the bone.
Nothing is safe before him. Whate'er he finds he takes.

Léandre :

Now, father, here's a case for you.   But mercy sakes!
Put yourselves after him!   Run, all!

Dandin :

Not so much clatter;
Softly; an apprehension private suits this matter.

Léandre :

Father, make an example worthy of belief;
Punish with severity this domestic thief.

Dandin :

But I wish to try the case with due formality;
Counsel should be assigned, for impartiality;
But we have none.

Léandre :

Ah, well, it self-defense is
T' appoint your porter and amanuensis.
I think you'll make of each an excellent advocate —
They are quite ignorant.

L'Intimé :

How wrong! for with a state
Of drowsiness I can a judge as soon infect
As any one.

Petit-Jean :

As I know naught, nothing expect.

Léandre :

This being your first case, it shall be well prepared.

Petit-Jean :

But I can't read at all.

Léandre :

A prompter 'll give the word.

Dandin :

Now let us go prepare.   And, gentlemen, no chicane :
We close our eyes to bribes, to our ears intrigue is
     vain.
 Master Little-John the complainant represents ;
You, Master L'Intimé, appear for the defense.

ACT THIRD.

SCENE I.

CHICANEAU, LÉANDRE, PROMPTER.

Chicaneau:

Yes, this is the way, sir, they manage each affair;
I know not either bailiff nor commissioner.
Every word I tell you's true.

Léandre:

I believe it all;
But if you'll credit me, you'd better let it fall.
It is in vain to think of prosecuting both;
To trouble your repose as well as their's you're loth.
Already you have spent three-fourths of your estate,
Bags heaped on one another with papers to inflate;
And all in this pursuit against your interest.

Chicaneau:

That your advice is good is certainly confessed,
And I intend ere long your counsel to pursue.
But first, with intercession, try what I can do.
Soon as his honor Dandin gives an audience,
I will bring my daughter with greatest diligence.
She's very truthful; let them interrogate her;
And even than myself she will answer better.

Léandre:

Go and return again. You shall have justice done.

Prompter:

Oh, what a man!

Léandre :

I use a strange deception,
But father is a man driven to desperation ;
We'll amuse him with a case in imagination.
I have another wish, and that's for condemnation
Of this mad fool who brings all into litigation.
But look you, close upon our heels come in our mates.

SCENE II.

DANDIN, LÉANDRE ; L'INTIMÉ AND PETIT-JEAN in
gowns ; THE PROMPTER.

Dandin :

Come, who are you down there ?

Léandre :

These are the advocates.

Dandin, to the Prompter :

And you ?

Prompter :

I come to help their halting memory.

Dandin :

I understand.   And you ?

Léandre :

I'm the auditory.

Dandin :

Commence then.

Prompter :

Gentlemen —

Petit-Jean:
Oh, take a lower key,
For if you prompt so loud they never can hear me.
My lord —

Dandin:
Put on your hat.*

Petit-Jean:
Oh, sir —

Dandin:
I say put on your hat.

Petit-Jean:
Oh, sir, I think I understand good breeding better'n
that.

Dandin:
Then don't put on your hat.

Petit-Jean, putting on his hat, to Prompter:
Well, Prompter, now be dumb;
That which I know the best is my exordium.
Your honors, when I consider with exactitude
The world's inconstancy, full of vicissitude;
When I behold so many races different,
So many wandering stars, not one star permanent;
When I view Cæsar and consider his fortune;
When I behold the sun, when I behold the moon;
When I behold the state of the Babylonians,
Transferred from Persia to the Macedonians;
When I behold the Lorraines, at first despotical,
Pass to a democracy, then grow monarchical;
When I behold Japan —

---

* The French lawyers were privileged to plead covered.

L'Intimé :
When will he stop beholding ?

Petit-Jean :
Oh dear ! why will he interrupt me with his scolding ?
I cannot speak a word.

Dandin :
Restive attorney,
Why don't you let him finish up his journey ?
When I'm a-sweat to learn if he'n Japan discover
A harbor for his capon, and thus his wandering's over,
You've interrupted him with your discourse absurd.
Now, advocate, proceed.

Petit-Jean :
I can't.   I've lost the word.

Léandre :
Out with it, Little-John.   Your *début* none derides.
But why d'ye keep your arms stuck close against your
    sides ?
And stand upon your feet like a statue perpendicular ?
Come, brighten up, don't be afraid, we're not particular.

Petit-Jean, moving his arms :
When — I behold — when — I behold —

Léandre :
Well, what ? you dunce ?

Petit-Jean :
Why, how can one expect to course two hares at once ?

Prompter :
'Tis said —

Petit-Jean :
"Tis said—

Prompter :

In the —

Petit-Jean :

In the —

Prompter :

Metamorphosis —

Petit-Jean :

What say ?

Prompter :

That the metem —

Petit-Jean :

That the metem —

Prompter :

Sychosis —

Petit-Jean :

Sychosis —

Prompter :

Oh dear ! The horse —

Petit-Jean :

The horse —

Prompter :

Again said !

Petit-Jean :

Again —

Prompter :

The dog —

Petit-Jean :

The dog —

Prompter :

Oh blockhead !

9

Petit-Jean :

     The blockhead —

Prompter :

Plague take this advocate !

Petit-Jean :

     The plague on you be cast !
See t'other fellow, too, with's face like Lenten fast !
Go to the devil, all !

Dandin :

    Come, on to business push.

Petit-Jean :

Oh dear me ! what's the use of beating round the
  bush ?
They teach me to speak words in length a fathom
  each,
Big sounding words, that would from here to Pontoise
  reach.
Now, I don't see the sense of all this hurly-burly ;
In short to find a fowl I came this morning early ;
There's naught your dog won't steal, if it but take the
  shape on
Of fowl, and now he's gone and gobbled up our capon—
A capon from the Maine ; here's nothing to decide ;
The first time that I catch him, I'll soundly tan his hide.

Léandre :

A very neat conclusion, worthy your setting out !

Petit-Jean :

Oh, carp who will. One knows my meaning without
  doubt.

Dandin :

Produce your witnesses.

Léandre :

Well said, if he's got any.
They don't come for the wish; they cost a deal of money.

Petit-Jean :

We have a plenty, though, and they're beyond reproach.

Dandin :

Let them present themselves.

Petit-Jean :

I have them in my pouch.
Behold them! here they are—the capon's legs and head!
Examine them and judge.

L'Intimé :

I object to them.

Dandin :

Well said!
But why object?

L'Intime :

They're from the Maine;* their trade's to cozen.

Dandin :

True, these Maine witnesses crowd in here by the dozen.

L'Intimé :

Your honor—

Dandin :

Tell me, sir, shall you be expeditious?

---

* I infer that the inhabitants of Maine were notorious "experts."

L'Intimé :

I cannot answer any thing.

Dandin :

Why, that's judicious.

L'Intimé, in a tone ending in a squeal :

My lords, all that can astound the culpable,
All that which mortals hold the most redoubtable,
Against us here assembled, seems to be in league;
In short, I mean to say, eloquence and intrigue.
The fame of the deceased on one hand stands t' admonish,
On t' other, eloquence doth equally astonish,—
The shining eloquence of master Little John.

Dandin :

Say, can't you soften down the shrillness of your tone?

L'Intimé, in his ordinary voice :

Oh, yes, I've many of them. (*In a pompous tone :*)
Whatever diffidence
May justly be aroused by said fame and eloquence,
We rest upon your truth, as Hope leans on the anchor,
And trust your sense of right to mitigate all rancor.
Before the great Dandin innocence is power;
Yes, before the Cato of Normandy the Lower,
That sun of equity whose beams have never languished.
Vict'ry delights the gods; but Cato's for the vanquished.

Dandin :

Now truly he pleads well.

L'Intimé :

To make no further pause,
I take my cue, and go to the merits of my cause.
Aristotle wisely says, in his Politikon,—

Dandin :

Why, advocate, the point is now about a capon,
And not of Aristotle's views political.

L'Intimé :

But the authorities Peripatetical
Have proved that good and evil—

Dandin :

In courts of equity
Your Aristotle hasn't the least authority.
Come, to the point.

L'Intimé :

Pausanias, in his Corinthiacs,—

Dandin :

To the point.

L'Intimé :

Rebuffe—

Dandin :

To the point, I tell you.

L'Intimé :

The great Jacques—

Dandin :

The point, the point, the point!

L'Intimé :

Harmenopul, in fact,—

Dandin :

I'll render judgment now.

L'Intimé :

Oh dear, how rash you act.
Then have the facts. (*Quickly.*) This dog to the kitchen
    drawing nigh,
A capon plump and sweet within he did espy;

Now he for whom I speak with hunger there was
 hasting;
He against whom I speak was nicely plucked and
 basting;
Then he for whom I speak, seized on, took off, secreted
Him against whom I speak. The larder thus depleted,
He's take on a writ. Counsel plead pro and con;
A day's fixed. I'm to speak, I speak, and now I've
 done.

Dandin :

Tut, tut, tut, tut! Learn better how to try your case.
Th' irrelevant you give at a deliberate pace,
Th' important you run over at a gallop strong.

L'Intimé :

The former, may it please you, sir, is fine.

Dandin :

        It's wrong.
Were causes ever known to be in this way pleaded?
What say th' assembly?

Léandre :

    This style is now most heeded.

L'Intimé, in a vehement tone :

Where were we, gentlemen? They come. And how
 come?
They chase my client, and they force a mansion.
What mansion? Why, the mansion of our own judge.
They force the cellar which serves us for refuge.
Of brigandage they then accuse us, and of theft,
We're then dragged headlong forth, and to our accus-
 ers left,

To master Little John, your honor—I attest.
Who does not know the law, If any Dog (Digest
De vi, and see the paragraph *Caponibus*),
Is manifestly contrary to such abuse?
And when it turned out true that my poor client Citron
Had eaten all or most of the aforesaid capon,
Against this trifling deed you will not hesitate
To weigh our former actions, and let them mitigate.
When has my client ever been reprimanded?
By whom has this your house always been defended?
When have we failed to bark at robbers in our town?
Witness three low attorneys, from whom we've torn
    the gown.
They show you certain fragments to accuse us by;
Receive these other fragments to help us justify.

Petit-Jean :

But Adam—

L'Intimé :

You keep still.

Petit-Jean :

L'Intimé—

L'Intimé :

You're too rude.

Petit-Jean :

He 's hoarse!

L'Intimé :

Shut up!

Dandin :

Repose a moment, then conclude.

L'Intimé, in a wheezing voice :

Since, then, a moment's rest to catch our breath 's
    permitted,

And formal peroration 's to be intermitted,
I come, without omission or prevarication,
Compendiously t' enunciate an explication,
And hold up to your eyes a general exposition
Of all my cause, and all my client's imposition.

Dandin :

T' repeat the same thing twenty times, he prefers by
    far,
Than once t' abridge. Oh, man, or whatever else you
    are,
Devil, conclude; or heav'n seize thee with damnation!

L'Intimé :

I finish now.

Dandin :

      Oh!

L'Intimé :

      Before the world's creation —

Dandin :

Oh, skip over to the flood!

L'Intimé :

      Well, then, before the birth
Of time, of the material system, and of earth,—
The world, the universe, and nature universal,
Lay buried in the bosom of the material.
The elements,—the fire, the earth, the air, the water,—
Piled up or buried, are nought but heaps of matter,
A dire confusion, a mass of matter formless,
Chaos, disorder, and brooding rout enormous.
As Ovid sings, there was, on all the face of nature,—
Called chaos by the Greeks — one rude indefinite
    feature.

(Dandin, being sleepy, nods and falls heavily.)

Léandre :

My father, what a tumble !

Petit-Jean :

See how he drops his head !

Léandre :

Come, father, rouse yourself !

Petit-Jean :

Your honor, are you dead ?

Léandre :

Father ! I say.

Dandin :

Well, well ? what ? who ? a man, it seems.
Truly, I've been asleep, and had quite pleasant dreams.

Léandre :

Come, sir, decide.

Dandin :

To the galleys !

Léandre :

You hardly can, sir,
Punish a dog that way.

Dandin :

No more—you have my answer.
What with the world and chaos, I've such a muddled
    pate !
Wind up this cause.

L'Intimé, presenting the puppies to him :

Come hither, you family desolate ;
Come, little ones, whom he would orphans render,
Give utterance to your understandings tender.

10

Yes, gentlemen, you here behold our misery;
Restore a father to his orphan'd family;
Our father dear, by whom we were engender'd —
Our father dear —

Dandin :

This issue can't be tender'd.

L'Intimé :

Our father, gentlemen —

Dandin :

Don't keep up such discord.
They're making a great muss —

L'Intimé :

Behold our tears, my lord !

Dandin :

Why, now, I seem to be quite taken with compassion ;
O what a thing to touch the feelings in this fashion !
I am quite bothered here. The fact alleged so presses ;
A crime's averred ; th' accused himself confesses.
But if he is condemned, equal's th' embarrassment.
For then these pretty children must be to th' asylum
   sent.
But I can't see a person. I am occupied.

SCENE III.

DANDIN, LÉANDRE, CHICANEAU, ISABELLE,
L'INTIMÉ, PETIT-JEAN.

Chicaneau :

Sir—

Dandin :

Court for you is open, and for none beside.
Adieu—but who is that young lady going thither?

Chicaneau :

That is my daughter, sir.

Dandin :

Quick! go and call her hither.

Isabelle :

But you are occupied.

Dandin :

I've nothing to do more.
(*To Chicaneau:*) If she's your child, sir, why not
tell me so before?

Chicaneau :

My lord—

Dandin :

Better than you she knows where merit lies.
Say—but she is pretty, and then what tender eyes!
But that's not all, my child, prudence is required.
To see such youthfulness I am with joy inspired.
D'ye know that I was formerly a gay young beau?
We have been talked about.

Isabelle :

You must have been, I know.

Dandin :

Tell us, whom would you like to cause to lose his
    action ?

Isabelle :

No one.

Dandin :

    But speak.   You can imagine no exaction
I'd not perform.

Isabelle :

        You oblige me, sir, too much, in fact.

Dandin :

Have you, for instance, never seen a person racked ?

Isabelle :

No, and believe I never would for my salvation.

Dandin :

I wish you'd gratify for this your inclination.

Isabelle :

Oh, when th' unhappy suffer, can any one stand by ?

Dandin :

Why, to fill an hour or two, it answers passably.

Chicaneau :

Sir, I've come here to say to you —

Léandre :

             Now, in a word,
Sir, I'll explain to you the whole affair you've heard.
It is about a marriage.   And to begin, 'tis due
To tell you all's arranged, and now depends on you.
The lady wishes it; the lover, too, is sighing ;
And what the lady wishes, the father is desiring.
It is for you to judge.

Dandin :

Marry at once, I say;
To-morrow, if you wish it; if need be, to-day.

Léandre :

Your father in the law, Miss—come hither, this is he.
Salute him.

Chicaneau :

How is this?

Dandin :

What is the mystery?

Léandre :

That which you have said, perform, and not undo it.

Dandin :

Since, then, I have decided, I'll not review it.

Chicaneau :

Young ladies are not given without their own consent.

Léandre :

Doubtless; to charming Isabelle to leave it, I'm content.

Chicaneau :

Art thou then silent? Come, now, speak, it is for
    thee
To speak.

Isabelle :

I dare not, father, appeal from the decree.

Chicaneau :

But I appeal myself.

Léandre, showing him a paper :

Behold this writing. You're
Not going to appeal from your own signature?

Chicaneau :

What's this?

Dandin :

It is a contract that cannot be impeached.

Chicaneau :

But I will be revenged.   I have been overreached.
Of more than twenty law-suits this will be the source.
He's got the daughter—well !   He shall not have the
  purse.

Léandre :

O sir, who says we looked for money when we sought
  her ?
Keep your goods and welcome, but leave to us your
  daughter.

Chicaneau :

Ah !

Léandre :

Sir, are you pleased with the sessions' termination ?

Dandin :

Indeed I am.   But give me scope for litigation,
And pass the rest of life with you I would as lief.
But let the barristers in future be more brief.
And now our criminal ?

Léandre :

              Let all in joy be merged.
Pardon, father, pardon :

Dandin :

              Well, let him be discharged.
Daughter in law, I do this only for your sake.
In view of other trials, let us respite take.

NOTE. — That *L'Intimé's* rhetoric is not without a parallel in more recent times, is evident from the following extract, from the sketch of Lord Tenterden, in Townsend's *Lives of Twelve Eminent Judges :*

"One day in banc a learned gentleman, who had lectured on the law, and was too much addicted to oratory, came to argue a special demurrer. 'My client's opponent,' said the figurative advocate, 'worked like a mole under ground, *clam et secrete.*' His figures and law-Latin only elicited an indignant grunt from the chief justice. 'It is asserted in Aristotle's Rhetoric—' 'I do n't want to hear what is asserted in Aristotle's Rhetoric,' interposed Lord Tenterden. The advocate shifted his ground, and took up, as he thought, a safe position. 'It is laid down in the Pandects of Justinian—' 'Where are you got now?' 'It is a principle of the civil law—' 'Oh, sir!' exclaimed the judge, with a tone and voice which, to a punster's ear, would have abundantly justified his assertion; 'we have nothing to do with the civil law in this court.'"